Barbie Loves
Ballet

By Angela Roberts • Illustrated by Karen Wolcott

A Random House PICTUREBACK® Book
Random House 🏠 New York

BARBIE and associated trademarks and trade dress are owned by, and used under license from, Mattel, Inc.
Copyright © 2005, 2009 Mattel, Inc. All Rights Reserved.
Published in the United States by Random House Children's Books, a division of Random House, Inc., 1745
Broadway, New York, NY 10019, and in Canada by Random House of Canada Limited, Toronto. No part of this book may
be reproduced or copied in any form without permission from the copyright owner. Pictureback, Random House, and the
Random House colophon are registered trademarks of Random House, Inc. Originally published separately in different
form by Random House Children's Books, a division of Random House, Inc., New York, in 2005.
Library of Congress Control Number: 2008937007   ISBN: 978-0-375-85148-3
www.randomhouse.com/kids   MANUFACTURED IN CHINA   10 9 8 7 6 5 4 3 2

"Remember to keep your toes pointed!" said Kelly's dance teacher, Miss Lee. "Keep your backs straight, and don't forget to smile!"

Kelly didn't have to be reminded to smile. She loved everything about ballet—the music, the steps, and especially the spins!

"Next week, we're going to have a recital!" said Miss Lee. "All your friends and family can come to see you dance."

Everyone cheered—everyone, that is, except Kelly.

"I heard that you're going to have a recital," Barbie said when she picked up her little sister after class. "I'm going to be there, too. Miss Lee asked me to help all of you get ready and to perform one of my ballet routines. Won't it be fun?"

DANCE STUDIO

BALLET
LESSONS

"I don't want to be in the recital," Kelly said.

"Why not?" Barbie asked. "You love ballet, and you're so good at it!"

"I do love ballet," Kelly agreed, "but I don't want to dance in front of all those people. I might mess up or stumble and fall down!"

Kelly practiced after school and after dinner.

"You were right, Barbie," Kelly said. "I've practiced so much that I'm not nervous at all."

The big day finally arrived! At the ballet studio, everyone rushed to get ready.

"Has anyone seen my ballet shoes?" asked Lexie.

"Can someone comb my hair?" asked Chloe.

"I'm scared," Kelly said as Barbie helped her get dressed. "I feel like I have butterflies in my stomach—even after all that practice."

"Everyone gets butterflies," said Barbie, "but after all your hard work, you can go out there knowing that you're ready to do your very best!"

After Barbie finished helping everyone get into their costumes, she went onstage and danced for the crowd. The audience loved it!

Then it was Kelly's turn. She leaped and turned and danced in perfect time to the music. Kelly had practiced so much, she hardly had to think about her routine. Her feet knew just what to do!

As the dancers ended their routine, the audience jumped to their feet.

"Bravo! Bravo!" everyone shouted.

"You were great out there!" Barbie said to Kelly backstage. "All your hard work really paid off."

"Thanks!" Kelly said. "You were great, too. And thanks for helping me practice. I'm going to keep on working hard so I can be a great ballerina!"

Barbie smiled. "You know what, little sister?" she asked. "You already are!"

The next day, Barbie and Kelly were the hit of the fashion show.

"We make a great team," Barbie said.

"We sure do!" agreed Kelly.

"Kelly was great," Joanne said. "And I'd love it if you were *both* in the fashion show tomorrow."

"Wow!" Barbie and Kelly said together.

"That was wonderful!" Barbie said to all the children after the show.

"It sure was," said Joanne, the fashion show organizer. "I really liked your dress-up fashion show."

"Thanks," said Barbie. "It was a lot of fun."

"Next we have Kelly dressed as a ballerina," said Barbie. Kelly walked in front of the curtain and twirled around in her tutu. The audience applauded and Kelly curtsied for them.

"Here is Karen dressed as a princess," Barbie announced to the audience. Everyone cheered for Karen as she came out from behind the curtains.

The day of the big show, Barbie cued Tommy to open the curtains. Then she turned on some music and the fashion show began!

The next day, the girls gathered in Barbie's backyard to try on their outfits. Everyone was very excited!

"We're all set," Barbie said. "We can have the fashion show this weekend. Here are invitations for your families."

Later that day, Kelly looked in her closet for something to wear.

"How about this?" Kelly asked as she put on a pretty pink top and a tutu.

"That's perfect!" Barbie said. "And you can borrow my necklace to go with your outfit."

Kelly loved to see Barbie all dressed up.

"Can *we* put on a dress-up fashion show?" asked Kelly.

"Sure," said Barbie. "Why don't you call your friends to see if they want to be in it, too?"

Kelly couldn't wait!

had her hair styled . . .

and picked out different pieces
of jewelry to wear for the show.

Barbie tried on lots of pretty outfits . . .

"Yay, Barbie!" Kelly cheered as she watched her sister rehearse for a fashion show.

"That was great, Barbie," said Joanne, the fashion show organizer. "Now it's time for a wardrobe change."

"Sure thing," said Barbie as she went backstage.

You are cordially invited to The First Annual Neighborhood Fashion Show

Date: SATURDAY
Place: BARBIE'S BACKYARD
Time: 11:00 AM

Fashion Show *Fun!*

By Mary Man-Kong • Illustrated by Karen Wolcott

A Random House PICTUREBACK® Book
Random House 🏠 New York